In The Name Of Love

Kumar Vikrant

Delhi - 110089, India

Edition : 2020
ISBN : 978-93-89984-00-2

In The Name Of Love
By : Kumar Vikrant

Published by
Prakhar Goonj Publication
H-3/2, Sector - 18,
Rohini, Delhi - 110089
Contact : 7982710571, 7838505899, 011-27851059

Email : prakhargoonj@gmail.com
     sinha.neelu123@gmail.com

This book is for my daughter Arohi,
who always inspires me to write more.

Preface

Sometimes I think about the news paper clip which I came across in the summer of 2010, the news paper clip was about the contract killers who were being used by the Mumbai underworld to spill a lot of bad blood. Soon I was reading a lot about the contract killers and came to a conclusion that killing people for money was their way of earning their living, and only the best survives in this field. And that is how my first story 'A Clean Hit,' came into existence and gained a lot of positive and negative criticism. After this story I wrote a number of stories based on the true crimes. It was the beginning of my literary journey. 'In The Name Of Love,' is also based on a true crime which took place a few years ago at a shopping mall in my hometown. A beautiful woman was teased physically by a khadi clad degenerated politician and when her husband intervened, he was beaten by the henchmen of that politician. Later the security guards saved that poor man but the damage was done and I was forced to think that how a powerful man can destroy the happy life of any ordinary family.

Any way writing this book was really a tedious task for me but some people who play important part in my life helped me all through the journey of this book.

My kid daughter Arohi; who don't let me sleep until I tell her a story. She doesn't have any idea what is this book about but she always asks me tell the stories related to this book.

My wife Ranjita who has always been a very big critic of my stories; she went on bearing it with me and my continues typing on computer until the book was complete.

My friend Shalini Dikshit who is also a very good

writer; didn't rest until I send the manuscript of this book to the publisher. She never failed to inquire the day by day progress of the book, if I ever procrastinated in any matter of this book, she went on inquiring until I completed that matter.

Thanks, guys, for your heartfelt help.

I'm thankful to my friend Raj Verma, my cousin Aishwarya Raghav and niece Shruti Singh; they have always been the first readers of and admirers of my stories.

Kumar Vikrant
01/03/2020

In The Name Of Love

August 14th, 10:30 AM

The lady jailer gave her necessary instructions and handed over her belongings which Seema put in a small satchel. Zoura jail was the only women's jail in the northern region and it was the most notorious jail too for various reasons. The jail was situated 10 km south of Junagarh near Zoura village. Seema was shifted here from Veer Nagar to serve her three- and half-year term. She glanced at the administrative block and walked towards the main entrance.

The male sentry opened the little passage through the big main gate of the jail. He also told her that she could hire a cab to Junagarh and from there she could get any public transport to go anywhere she wanted to go. She came out of the gate and didn't speak a single word to thank him. The road outside was empty, there was not a single soul to welcome her out of the jail and she was not expecting one. She decided to walk towards the city. It was early morning, but the weather was hot and humid. She looked around, but there was no public or private vehicle, she walked ahead again. Suddenly she heard the screeching sound of an auto rickshaw engine somewhere behind her; she turned back and waved to stop the auto rickshaw.

"Going to the city?" asked the rickshaw driver.

She nodded and took the back seat of the rickshaw.

"From Zoura?" asked the driver while accelerating the vehicle.

She ignored him and kept quiet.

"A real tough place." sighed the driver.

Earlier on August 13th

1

The secretary entered the room of state minister of women and child welfare, Ranjit after knocking it.

"What is it?" frowned the man sitting behind the big wooden table.

"Sorry sir, Peter wants to meet you."

"Send him in."

Ranjit was a big man in all aspects. Six feet plus tall, burly body, though in his mid-forties, but there was no gray hair on his head. There were several gold chains hanging around his neck. There was another gold chain wrapped around his wrist. All his ten fingers were full of rings; there were some stone studded rings amongst the rings.

Minister Ranjit was a bit frustrated today. He tried his best in the high court of the northern region to get her punished with life imprisonment or at least a sentence of ten years for the attempt on his life by her. But the Judge Tripathi bench didn't budge a little to his political pressure and he punished her with four years' imprisonment. Another bench reduced her punishment to three and half years. And to his surprise, she was about to release just after three years and half years' imprisonment at Zoura jail.

He silently cursed the day when he first saw Seema at the Veer Nagar city mall. He was so moved by her beauty that he couldn't controll himself and went forward to hold her hand in public. She slapped his face and in response he kicked her in her belly. She cried like a mad woman, her husband also rushed at him, his henchmen tried to hold him back, but the man was very strong and he broke away from their grip and came straight to him.

Fortunately, or unfortunately he had his gun with him on that day. He shot that madman before he could touch him. He was in a rage and he emptied his gun at the rushing man, the bullets didn't only kill the rushing man but wounded his son badly. He left the mall immediately and contacted his party leader and told him everything. The party leader scolded him mildly and advised him to surrender. Later, his party friends managed to get him out on bail. The media and Some NGO's started agitation all over the city and the media presented him as a monster who had destroyed a family by killing an innocent man.

Things became worse when the wounded child died in the hospital. The whole country was in turmoil and his bail was cancelled by the district judge and he was again back in jail. Finally, the trial of his case began and the trial was turning point of his life, his party leader fixed the judge and his lawyers proved that the murder was a sad culmination of the extra marital relation between Seema and Ranjeet. Somehow her husband Vinod came to know about it and couldn't control himself when he saw Ranjeet at the mall and attacked him. All Ranjeet did was not a violent act, but a self-defense.

The judge wrote a lengthy judgment and questioned on the marriage system which forced a woman and man to live in a false relationship. According to him Ranjeet was not an innocent man, but he was also not a murderer, the murder was a result of an illegitimate relationship and self-defense. He instructed government authorities to file a separate case on Seema and punished Ranjeet with a six months imprisonment without bail. He served six months in the Veer Nagar jail as a king with the blessing of his party leader.

On the day of his release from the jail, he was received

by his party leader and was taken to the party office like a political victim. There was a big press gathering at party office and the press conference began. There were questions from the newspapers and news channel correspondence which Ranjeet and his party leaders answered with a smile.

Suddenly Seema emerged from the press crowd and rushed towards the tables where Ranjeet was sitting with his allies. She jumped over the table and stabbed an iron rod in Ranjeet chest, which she was holding in her hand. Everyone was standstill in that conference room; Ranjeet had fallen on the floor and was bleeding profusely. Suddenly the party leader gained his senses and he shouted at his men, 'Idiots, what are you waiting for, kill that woman." All the party henchmen jumped at her and started kicking and dragging her.

Press people started shooting this interesting scene, but suddenly a police car pulled in and number of police men rushed in and warned people to stay away from Seema. Soon the situation was under control, wounded Ranjeet was sent to hospital and half dead Seema to the police station.

Ranjeet was badly wounded. His left lung was punctured by that iron rod and his heart was missed by a few centimeters. He spent three months in the hospital and he had to go through multiple surgeries during these months.

Government attorneys made a very strong case against Seema and demanded the death penalty for her. She didn't utter a single word during the trial and the judge concluded that the attempt on Ranjeet's life was an act of rage and there was a chance of improvement in Seema and he sentenced her four years imprisonment without bail. Ranjeet's people were furious, they appealed again, but their appeal was cancelled.

"Called me, sir?"

"Yes." Ranjeet came out of his reveries when he saw

Peter standing before him.

"They are releasing her tomorrow, make it sure that she must not leave Junagarh alive." he uttered by clenching his teethes.

"Should it look like an accident?"

"No, no, shoot her in public."

"Okay, as you wish."

Ranjeet waved him off.

2

Deputy Inspector General (DIG) Veer Nagar, Shahil Khan left his office in a hurry; Inspector General (IG) Will City Jeevan Anand wanted an urgent meeting with him at that very moment. Within two hours he was on the second floor of the police headquarter Will City, where the IG was waiting for him. When he entered in the IG room after knocking, the IG was scrolling something on his laptop.

Khan saluted him and the IG waved him to sit without raising his head. Suddenly he turned his laptop screen towards Khan. There was a woman's face flashing on the screen.

"Look at this face carefully." said the IG.

The face was really attractive in every aspect.

"This woman can create a lot of trouble in the near future here in the city." said the IG.

"Who is she?" asked Khan.

"Her name is Seema Singh; she is presently in Zaura prison serving her three- and half-year term." IG paused for a moment and went on again, "She is in prison for attacking Mr. Ranjeet, honorable minister, but due to some writs filed by various organizations, the honorable high court has reduced her prison term from four years to three- and half-year term, she may be released from the jail tomorrow."

"Do you think she will again make an attempt on the life of the minister?"

"Not sure, but during the trial she told the world that she will come back to kill him."

"And that is the anticipated trouble, according to you?' said Khan.

"No today is August thirteenth and she may be released tomorrow, ring something?"

"You mean there may be trouble on the parade ground in Veer Nagar on August 15th."

"Correct, the minister will be hoisting the national flag at 07:40 in the morning on the parade ground in Veer Nagar, and her presence out there might create a lot of trouble."

"What do you want me to do?" asked Khan.

"Get the best of your men and protect the minister, take a printout of the picture of this woman and circulate it on all the police check posts, increase the force on airport, railway station and bus stations."

"Okay."

"Arrest her if she tries to enter the city and bring her to me." said the IG.

"May I ask a question, sir?" said Khan to the IG.

"Sure, what is it?"

"Why does she want to kill him?"

"I just went through the news archives; papers say an illicit relationship between this woman and the minister was the reason of her husband and son's accidental murder."

"Accidental murder? Never heard this word composition." said Khan with a smile.

"These media people use such words, but it is written in police records that Mr. Ranjeet fired in self-defense and got that poor man killed."

"So, she wants to avenge her husband and son's death?" asked Khan.

"She was almost successful last time when she stabbed an iron rod in the chest of the minister, his wounds were fatal he could have died."

"Then I don't believe in the illicit relationship story, there is more behind this story." said Khan to himself.

"What?"

"Nothing, please go ahead, sir."

"Please don't let your personal interpretation rule over your brain, there is a dangerous woman in Zaura jail and she may be released in a day or two. And her presence in Veer Nagar may endanger the life of the minister and the peace of that city, got it."

"Yes, sir."

"Then make sure both the minister and the peace of Veer Nagar are secured."

"Yes, sir."

"Meeting is over."

3

"Zoya, as I remember you covered the Seema case from beginning to her imprisonment?" asked Atul Shah, the chief editor of City News Channel.

"Yes, I did, sir, is there anything new about her?" asked Zoya.

"You know she has been serving her three and half years' imprisonment in Zoura jail for three and half years."

"I know, sir."

"Please let me finish." said Atul and went on, "I have news that they are releasing her tomorrow."

"That is interesting." said Zoya.

"Don't you think she will attack Ranjeet again?"

"As far as I know about her, she'll never miss a chance to kill Ranjeet and her best chance is on August 15th when the minister will be in public, hoisting the national flag on parade ground of Veer Nagar."

"So, what are you waiting for, go ahead and work on this clue. I want some exclusive videos of her; we'll run her story in prime time today."

"Sure, sir, hope I'll get something new on her."

"That's good."

August 14th, 03:45 AM

Peter and Zagir reached at Junagarh early in the morning. They were dead tired after the ten hours driving from Veer Nagar to Junagarh. All they wanted was a little sleep. They decided to stay in a cheap motel with fake names and fake id's. There were several cheap motels in that small town and they hired the nearest of the Jail. They secured their weapons before going to bed, and set their mobile alarms at seven am.

August 14th, 10:32 AM

A sharp buzzing sound forced to wake Peter up. He rubbed his eyes and fished his mobile phone out of his pocket. He made more efforts to look at the phone screen which was flashing minister Ranjeet's number.

"Yes, sir."

"Work done?"

"We've reached at Junagarh; we'll get the work done before noon."

"This is before noon idiot, go and get her."

He glanced at his wrist watch, whose arms were displaying 10:32.

"Sorry sir, we are going…. just…about to leave…."

"Listen, you miss her today and you are a dead man."

Mobile phone went silent.

Peter kicked Jagir who was still sleeping and cursed himself. They left the motel in a hurry and rushed towards the Jail. Jagir was driving the car while Peter was loading his mouser. Soon the jail was in their sights.

The jail's main door was closed. There was not a single human being outside of the jail. Peter left the car and went straight to the jail door. He knocked the door, a sentry peeped through a small hole.

"What do you want?" inquired the sentry.

"Ugh… we came to receive, Seema ji, when will she be released?"

"You arc latc, she has been released." And the sentry closed the hole.

He was frustrated on the news; he saw in every direction helplessly, there was a tea vendor on the other side of the main door. He went towards him and asked, "Bhai, did you see a woman leaving the jail today?"

The tea vendor looked at his face with a little suspicion and said, "No, I didn't see any woman leaving the jail today."

Peter scratched his head and came back to his car.

"She has left." He said to Jagir and again cursed the alarm, which couldn't wake them.

"She must have taken a bus or some other public

In the name of love

transport." said Jagir.

"You are right, let's check the roadways stand and railway station."

August 14th, 11:38 AM

Seema left the auto at the main door of the roadways stand. She looked for an ATM; there were three at various directions around the roadways stand. She went to the nearest one and inserted the ATM card in the slot provided. She was wondering if her account was still active, but to her surprise ATM accepted the card. She withdrew some money and came out of the bus stand.

She went to a nearby saari shop and bought a few for her. One of the saaries was pink in color.

Later she went to the roadways station again. She went to inquire office and inquired about a bus towards Will City.

"There is no direct bus to Will City from here, take bus to Devdurg, which is the Junction city; you can get a bus to Will City from there." informed the clerk and said further, "Bus number 3024 is about to leave towards Devdurg.

She thanked the clerk and looked for the mentioned bus. There were not many buses at the time, she easily found the bus and as soon as she entered the bus the driver started the bus and accelerated it towards the main gate of the bus stand. She took the window seat; there were not many passengers in the bus. She looked outside; the bus was going through the narrow streets of Junagarh.

"Ticket ma'am!" the bus conductor interrupted her.

"One ticket…Devdurg."

"Three hundred five rupees."

In the name of love

The bus driver accelerated the bus to cover the 247 km distance between Junagarh and Devdurg.

August 14th, 12:14 PM

Jagir pulled in the car before the roadways stand. Peter came out of the car and glanced through the bus stand, there were a number of buses ready to leave for their destinations. He quickly checked every bus, but there was not a sign of Seema. They had lost her, he again cursed himself.

The humidity in the atmosphere was making him crazy; he wiped the sweat off his face and looked around. He saw the inquiry office and decided to give a try.

"Sir, we are looking for our sister, she has to go to Veer Nagar, do you remember any woman inquiring for a bus to Veer Nagar." asked Peter to the busy inquiry clerk.

"No, no one inquired about Veer Nagar." informed the clerk.

All of a sudden, his mobile started ringing, he fished out his phone. He was sad to see; minister number was again flashing on phone screen.

"Yes, sir."

"Found her, is she dead?"

"We lost her, sir."

"You useless burden, why the hell did I rely on you, idiot, find her, I'm warning you, if you don't find her, I'll send Jafar to find you."

Peter shivered at the mention of Jafar name, the ruthless contract killer who had never flunked a single killing contract.

"Sorry sir, we'll find her and inform you soon."

"You must."

And the phone screen went blank again.

August 14th, 12:30 PM

The bus was on the highway now and it was running at the maximum speed. Seema peeped through the window, there were vast agriculture fields, trees and spinney stretches all over. All these views may be beautiful for other people, but there was no beauty for her in this world. She saw her beautiful world shattering before her own eyes; she had criminated her husband and buried her three years old son. She still wonders how that fateful evening at the mall changed the course of her life.

She had earned a bad name for her; she was treated like an animal by the society after the media fortified her so called illicit relationship with that beast Ranjeet. She had never seen that animal of a man before that evening, but the nexus of police, media and judiciary labeled her a bad woman.

There was nothing much left in her life, she tried to kill that beast once, but that beast survived and she was punished.

Zoura jail had snatched whatever life was left in her, she had faced the worst of things at that place, but Devyani another inmate, eased her and inspired her to keep quiet and prepare herself for the revenge which was not taken yet. She also informed her that Ranjeet was a powerful man, he would not take any chance, and he would do his best to kill her. Thus, she knew the minister will also be waiting for her release to avenge the attack on his life by her. She knew he must be sending killers to kill her outside of Veer Nagar. So, going directly to Veer Nagar was not safe today that is why she decided to get into Veer Nagar via Will City, the adjacent city. Besides she wanted to meet an illegal arms merchant who could provide her a cheap gun. Most of all she wanted to meet Jack, the legendary warrior to help her in her revenge.

Seema, had no idea how to get near that Ranjeet, he was a minister in the state government now. It was very hard to break into his security, she had no resources, little money to buy any weapon, and she even had no place to live, no relatives left to shelter her. But August 15th, may be her chance when the minister may be in any public place to hoist the national flag.

Devyani also offered some outside help which Seema declined, but Devyani gave her the addresses of some people who could be helpful to her, Jack was among those people.

August 14th, 12:34 PM

Peter and Jagir gave a try at the railway station, but there was no direct train to Veer Nagar. There was one train in the evening, which used to go to Devdurg daily. They had lost Seema. There was a chance she might have hired a cab to Veer Nagar or she has sensed the danger and decided to go somewhere else. Finding her now was just like finding a needle in a hay heap.

There was not a single way to find her now; all the roads which reach Veer Nagar pass through Devdurg, so they must give a try to find her en route Devdurg or at Devdurg.

"Jagir, we are going to Devdurg, keep an eye on all the public and private vehicles."

"Sure boss." said Jagir and increased more pressure on the accelerator of the car.

August 14th, 05:45 PM

The journey was tiresome; the conductor stopped the bus almost at every small or big town so far. They even had a one-hour lunch break at a roadside Dhaba(Roadside restaurant). Passengers were coming into and going outside of the bus at every bus stand. Sometimes it was jammed with passengers and sometimes there were left only five to ten passengers. Seema napped a little occasionally and the heat outside wake her up abruptly.

Suddenly the bus slowed again and left the main road, after a few hundred yards there was a road side Dhaba named Greenway Hotel & Restaurant. There were several public and private vehicles gathered outside it and the passengers and staff of the buses were having some refreshment.

Seema came out of the bus and looked around, the place was filthy, and people were sitting on dirty tables, eating something. She looked for the washroom, which she found situated at the far corner. The washroom was filthy as well. She looked herself in the hazy mirror which was hung on the washroom wall, there was an unknown woman in the mirror, dark, aged, face full of wrinkles.

She came out of the washroom, went to the tea stall and ordered one cup of tea. She took a corner seat and sipped the tasteless tea.

The lazy bus drivers and conductors were resting after the refreshment. Their rest was boring for the passengers and some of the passengers were murmuring that they were getting late.

Finally, after a half hour long rest the driver of the bus came out of the Dhaba shelter, took his driving seat and started honking.

She moved towards her bus steadily, suddenly a car entered the Dhaba premise and came in between her and her bus.

August 14th, 06:17 PM

Jagir was driving the car at a very steady speed, fast but in control. En route Devdurg they came across several public and private transports, they tried to peep through them, but there was no sign of Seema. They were so disturbed by the minister warning that they even skipped their lunch. After a few hours driving they thought of eating something.

"I know a place where we could get something good for the lunch." said Jagir.

"Let's go there." agreed Peter.

After forty-five-minute journey they found the sign board of Greenway Hotel & Restaurant. Jagir slowed the car and entered the premises of the hotel. There were a number of parked vehicles; he looked for a place to park the car.

"Seema," whispered Peter in his ear.

Jagir saw, yes, she was walking in front of them. He stopped the car and let her go. She rushed towards a bus and vanished from their sight.

"We found her!" exclaimed Jagir.

"Yes, let the bus go and chase the bus at a very safe distance." instructed Peter.

"As you wish boss."

Jagir waited for a few moments and started chasing the bus cautiously.

Meanwhile, Peter called up the minister and informed him about finding Seema.

"Good, now give me the bus details, don't lose her now, I'm sending Jafar, kill her before he reaches otherwise, he will hunt you as well."

Peter gave the details of the bus and cursed the moment when he decided to take this job.

August 14th, 06:20 PM

Seema was astonished to see the men sitting in that car; she moved her face in the opposite direction and rushed towards her bus. There was something strange in the way they were looking at her. She took her seat and tried to control her breath.

Her instinct told her to look back. She left her seat and went to the back portion of the bus and peeped through the back window, yes, the car was behind the bus, chasing it.

She took her seat and closed the window. Milestone outside indicated Devdurg 47 km.

"So, the game has begun." murmured she.

She tilted a little behind and put her head on the cushion of the seat and closed her eyes, there was a strange smile on her blistered lips.

August 14th, 06:30 PM

Jafar turned off his computer. Rupees 50,00000 has been transferred to his account by his regular client, his client wanted to get a woman killed at any rate and that is why he agreed to pay such a big amount of money. Luckily, he had been staying in a small town called Koula situated fifty km east of Devdurg. He had to move fast, he wanted to finish the job outside of Devdurg.

He had recently killed Vakeel the main shooter of Bagga gang. He made that hit in Delhi, shooters of Bagga gang and Delhi police were looking for him. As usual, he was hiding in this remote place to let the heat settle down a little. He left his hiding place and checked his bag which contained his favorite rifle, Remington 700 XCR, rifle scopes for day and night vision, Colt 357 magnum revolver, and a long blade bowie knife. He placed the revolver under his arm, holster and knife in his long shoe's neck. He let the rifle and ammunition remained in the bag.

He was a strong man in every sense, six feet three inches tall, broad shoulders, strong jaws. He was 42 but looks older. He often put on formal clothes and had a businessman look on his face. Anyone who knew nothing about him would take him for a company executive. His look and dress sense always helped him to escape from a crime scene.

He came out of the narrow street and looked around like a hawk; there was none to take any interest in him. Outside on the road, he hired an auto rickshaw to Gogia Auto Garage, where he had left his Sedan car for service. His car required no service, but it was a safe way to hide his car. He often buys a different car for a new assignment, left it on any deserted road and hired a cab to escape from the crime place. But this assignment was given on such a short notice that he had no time to change this car.

In a few minutes he was in the garage, the owner of the garage was irritated to keep his car for a week long.

"Thank God, at last you came back, I was expecting that you'll never turn up." said the owner in a very angry tone.

"Sorry sir, I'm ready to pay the extra charges for keeping this car for me for such a long time," said Jafar with a little smile.

His softly spoken words were his perfect disguise. Anyone who talks to him would never think that he was talking to a ruthless killer, a killer who has never missed a hit.

He placed the bag on the back seat and started pushing the gas paddle in a perfect and steady way. Soon he was on the state highway and Devdurg was 45 km.

August 14th, 07:00 PM

"Will you ever learn to chase something?" said Peter with irritation.

"What's wrong?" asked Jagir

"You are trailing this bus like a rat; can't you overtake it?"

"Okay boss as you wish."

Jagir pumped more gas and overtook the bus with a little effort.

"Now look for a deserted place, we'll stop the bus to shoot her."

"How are we going to stop the bus?" asked Jagir.

"Have you got some brain or not? There are some narrow culverts, stop the car at any one of them, the bus driver will be forced to stop the bus. And that will be our chance to shoot her."

"Got it, you just tell me where to stop the car."

"Wait on I'm looking for the perfect culvert."

August 14th, 07:02 PM

Seema saw the car overtaking the bus.

So, they are going to stop the bus before Devdurg.

They are armed and dangerous, all the odds are against her, and she hasn't got a single stick with her to defend herself.

Stick, yes, there must be a leverage rod in the bus.

She knew they kept the rod at the driver's adjacent seat. She will have to rely on that rod, if there is one.

She kept her cool and waited.

August 14th, 07:05 PM

Sobha Singh was a bit frustrated today. The Senior Superintendent of Police didn't allot him women police station, she was made the in charge of Rural Area of Devdurg. And a junior sub inspector was appointed as the Station Head Officer of the women police station. Perhaps her notoriety as a tough woman had reached here before her arrival in Devdurg.

She joined the police by chance, she always wanted to join Indian Administrative Services, she tried her hard; she qualified pre and mains examination so many times but she always flunked the interview. After wasting all her attempts, she decided to give a try in state services, but again the same story, pre, main and fail. By chance state government announced vacancies of Sub Inspectors. Her friends advised her to give a try for she was tall and strong. She applied and went on qualifying and all the stages.

She joined the police department fifteen years ago at the age of 29. And at 44 today she had nothing in her hands, but two bad marriages, three suspensions, several departmental inquiries against her. Her reputation as a killer cop had closed all doors for her. Her way of interrogation was ruthless; there were two suicides, five deaths in lockup on her name now. No higher official was ready to take her at any city. She had always been posted at the worst police stations, criminals and corrupt policemen would try to leave that place for a better one.

She spent her first day at the police station by going through the files of the criminals of this area. Suddenly she got up and checked her mouser pistol and ordered her driver and follower to take her around the area and highway.

The driver told her that the police station Jeep was

out of order; the mechanic was checking the problem.

She frowned and ordered him to take her own car out. Soon they were on the highway. She told the driver that she would like to check the Naka police check post. The Naka police check post was notorious for the illegal activities of police men. It was situated at the highway at the 17th milestone. She wanted to catch them red handed.

After twenty minutes they were on a narrow culvert which was suitable only for one-way traffic. All of a sudden, the driver stopped the car as there was already a car and roadways bus on the culvert. The driver decided to remain on the other side of the culvert until the coming traffic pass.

August 14th, 07:20 PM

"Have you found them?"

"Who them?" asked Jafar.

"That woman, Peter and Jagir."

"I've not reached at Devdurg yet." said Jafar with irritation.

"Hope you'll inform me after getting her."

"You've given the job to me so trust me and never call back, I hate getting dictations, I'll get that woman." said he and disconnected the mobile phone.

He looked at the GPS, which was indicating that he was very close to his destination the city of Devdurg. He fished out his tablet computer and looked at the mug shot of Seema, provided by Ranjeet Dev. This time there was no clear plan to complete this hit. He had the bus details provided by his client, but he was also sure that the woman would hardly enter the city, if she was smart, she would not enter the city, she would elope in between the outer city and inner city. So, time was an important factor, he must catch the bus before she left it. So, he took a sharp turn and left the main road and took a paved road, this road would give him the benefit of 15 km. If everything went well, he would certainly get her before entering the main city.

August 14th, 07:25 PM

At the time of twilight Peter found the perfect culvert for the hold up. The weather was still hot and humid. He gave signal to Jagir. They entered the culvert; Peter saw the bus also followed them. Jagir waited until they reached the middle of the culvert then he stopped the big SUV.

Seema knew it was going to happen; she jumped from her seat and ran towards the driver and conductor seats. Luckily the leverage rod was lying under the conductor seat. She tilted a little and picked the rod.

Bewildered driver and conductor shouted simultaneously, "What are you doing.........?"

"Trouble." she said and pointed at the man who was coming out of that stopped SUV with a hand gun. Both the man left their seats and ran at the back side of the bus to find a hiding place. Their action created a panic among the passengers and they also ran towards the back seats of the bus.

Peter ran towards the main gate of the bus and kicked it to open it but it was locked inside. He ran towards the front glass screen of the bus; they were big enough to let a man enter into the bus. He looked for something to break the screen and he found a half brick on the road. He picked it and struck the screen with a vicious force, it shattered with an ear deafening sound and the glass scattered all over the road and inside the bus. He put a foot on the fender of the bus and sprang into the bus.

Seema saw the man entering the bus; she swung the rod towards him with a force. Peter tried to stand still in between the bonnet and side seat of the bus and he pulled out his gun from his belt where he crammed it before jumping into the bus. Before he could do anything, he saw an iron rod coming towards him, he retrieved his face but the rod struck his arm. The blow was unexpected and forceful, he lost his balance and the gun slipped from his hand.

Seema wanted to hit his head, but she missed it, but she had separated his gun from him. She swung the rod second time, but Peter not only saved him but jumped on her. They both tumbled down on the rough floor of the bus; peter managed to overcome her and subdued her with several powerful punches on her face.

She fell unconscious. Peter was looking for his gun, but there was no sign of it, he gritted his teeth kicked in her belly. Some passengers murmured, he raised his first finger towards them, looked at them with his fierce eyes, passengers ducked down. He looked at the wriggling Seema, he tilted down a little, held her by her hair and started dragging her towards the door of the bus. He opened the lock of the door, stepped down and dragged Seema with him.

He came out on the road and kicked again in the ribs of Seema, she cried aloud and he again kicked in her belly.

"Jagir!" Peter shouted.

The indication was enough for Jagir. He came out of the SUV with his gun and handed it over to Peter.

Half-conscious Seema opened her eyes, there was a dull figure of two men standing there, one of them was holding a gun in his hand. He turned towards her and fired at her.

"So, this is the end." thought Seema, she saw the flash of the gun barrel and turned around to dodge the bullet.

August 14th, 07:03 PM

The follower sitting in the front seat saw the hold up at the culvert. He waited for a while and saw all the action, a common Indian policeman habit. But when he saw that a man has dragged a woman out of the bus and was about to kill her, he shouted, "Ma'am trouble, shootout."

Shobha heard him and stammered abruptly, "Whaaa…. aat? Stop that!"

The follower jumped out of the car with his ancient police rifle, he wasn't sure if the rifle will be able to fire or not.

Shobha, pulled out his service revolver and ran towards the culvert where there were two armed men and a woman lying on the road. She suddenly heard the sound of gunfire.

She ran towards them, shot a fire in the air and shouted, "Police, leave the woman, drop your gun."

Peter missed his first fire; the woman writhed like a fish and dodged the bullet. Before he could fire again, he saw two policemen and police woman running towards them.

"What the hell………." he cursed and shouted at Jagir, "Take care of the police, I'll finish her off."

Fire sound has awakened Seema. She saw that her assailant was distracted; she gathered all her strength and kicked the gunman. Peter wobbled and shouted, "You… …I'll kill you."

Shobha saw the fallen woman. The man was again going to fire at the woman. It seemed that he wasn't much worried about the police. Shobha, sensed the situation, she aimed her gun towards the man's gun and fired.

Peter fired again at Seema, but a hot bullet hit his gun which fell down and his hand was wounded.

Peter looked at Jagir, who was standing like a fool.

"Run idiot." Peter shouted at Jagir. Jagir came out of the shock and they both ran towards their SUV.

Shobha saw them running towards their SUV, she didn't want to waste more bullets at them.

She shouted, "Stop…...or I'll shoot."

But both of them have entered their SUV, Jagir pushed the accelerator pumped gas and ran over the police people.

Shobha saw them entering their car and running towards her like a bullet, she jumped aside to save her. Both of his policemen also did the same. The big car was out of sight soon.

"Did you note the number of that car?" said Shobha to her policemen.

"Missed that." said the follower.

"Damn it, inform all the petrol cars, and tell them the car description." she instructed them.

Seema saw the entire violent episode. She got up and started moving towards the bus, but she saw a big policewoman walking towards her.

"O Madam, where are you going? What the hell was this? Who were they? Why were they trying to kill you? Shobha asked all the questions to her. Shobha went very close to Seema and held her by her arm. "Will you answer my questions here or need police station hospitality?"

Shobha looked at the terrified passengers and bus staff; she thought for a moment and waved them to go ahead.

The bus was gone.

August 14th, 08:00 PM

It was dark outside of the Naka police check post. The in charge of the check post Ojha was ordering a home guard to bring cold drinks for the police station staff. He was surprised to see SHO Shobha, who came to this check post with another woman. Shobha ordered him to stay outside.

Shobha went through the small cloth satchel which she found with Seema. There was nothing much, an ages old woman dress, a pink saree, an ATM card and discharge certificate for the Zaura jail.

"Seema? So, your name is Seema, a jail bird?" said Shobha with her harsh voice.

Seema kept quiet.

"Why did you go to the jail?"

There was no answer.

"O madam, I'm talking to you, speak up."

There was still the silence.

Shobha frowned.

Suddenly the check post in charge Ojha interrupted.

"Madam, this is Seema, she attacked Dev Saab."

"The minister, Ranjeet Dev?"

"Yes, madam. The men who attacked her must have been sent by him."

"Shut up Ojha, he is our honorable minister, we cannot allege him for this attack, and those ruffians must have something to do with her from her past life."

Ojha kept quiet for a while and then blurted, "Madam, we don't have anything against this woman, we must let her go otherwise minister Saab will send more goons, they shall massacre us all."

"Ojha, be in your limit."

"I know my limits ma'am, but I also know our

honorable minister, this woman is in a grave danger and her presence will endanger our lives too."

Suddenly she saw a paper which might have fallen from the satchel of that woman. She unfolded the paper. There were three words scribbled in blue ink.

'JACK WILL CITY'

"What is this?" Shobha inquired.

Seema maintained her silence.

"Ma'am, this woman has a very short life to live, the minister won't spare her." Ojha interrupted again.

Shobha looked at him irritatingly and pondered over the matter. There was nothing against her to detain her, she was the attack victim. And whatever Ojha saying was true, there may be trouble. She also knew about the criminal background of that minister, there may really be trouble. Let her die. Sure, what is wrong? People are born and found dead every day; she is not an exception. She may die, but not under her jurisdiction. Let her die at any other SHO's jurisdiction.

"Deepak." she called, her driver.

"Yes, madam." Deepak came rushing into the room.

"Take her with you to the city and leave her wherever she wants to go."

"*Ji madam* (sure madam), said Deepak and looked at Seema with disgust.

"*Aaja.* "(Come) said the driver to Seema.

Seema got up like a robot and followed the driver to the SHO's car.

"*Kaha Jayegi?* " (Where do you want to go?) Said the driver after starting the car.

"Bus stand." said Seema briefly.

August 14th, 09:00 PM

Jafar entered the city of Devdurg. It was dark everywhere, there was some sort of light failure in that area. There were only a few houses illuminated, perhaps due to any electric generating device. He fished out his cell phone and searched for Peter number, provided by Ranjeet Dev. After a brief searching, he found the number and dialed.

"Who is there?" a tired voice came from the other end.

"Where is that woman?" said Jafar without giving heed to the question.

"We have lost her, the police attacked us and we lost her." voice came from the other end, perhaps the man at the other end understood, who he was talking to.

"Give me the police men's description,"

"There were two male policemen and a female police inspector."

"A very huge woman?"

"Yes."

"Okay, now you are out of this case, don't mess with me anywhere." warned Jafar and disconnected the phone.

August 14th, 09:05 PM

Peter was terrified to hear the hissing voice of that ruthless killer. He saw the phone was disconnected. He heaved. He saw his wounded hand. Jagir had dressed his wound by using the first aid kit, which he had in the car.

Peter thought of the Ranjeet Dev's menace in case of failure, and he has been failed, failed very badly.

Suddenly he remembered that his gun was lying

somewhere in that cursed bus, if someone has not stolen it. The rupees 500000 cost gun had lost, his dear gun was lost.

"Jagir, we must check that bus, hope the gun is still in that bus."

"Who knows? Perhaps the bus has left for another destination."

"May be, but what's wrong if we give a try."

"As you wish boss, but remember people might recognize us."

"There is dark outside, no one will recognize us."

"Okay, let's go."

Soon they were inside the Bus stand. There were not so many buses out there at this hour. They looked for that bus; but there was no sign of that bus. Peter went to the inquiry; there was none in the inquiry box. But there was a bus conductor.

Peter went to him and asked, "Brother we came from Junagarh and we forgot our things in that bus, how can we find that bus?"

"Very hard, if the bus has gone back to Junagarh then you must go back to Junagarh to find your things. Besides please go and check at the bus depot, perhaps they have left the bus there before going elsewhere."

"Thanks a lot sir. I'll go and check the bust at the depot."

The bus depot was just beside the stand and the depot was mainly the workshop where they usually fix minor and major technical issues of the buses.

There was darkness everywhere. The bus was found easily both of them recognized it from its broken glass screen. Peter went into the bus stealthily and started searching for his gun with the help of a pencil torch. He searched every nook and corner of the bus, but the gun had vanished there was nothing but a lot of broken glass.

He clinched his teeth and cursed the whole world.

Suddenly the sound of several sirens panicked him, a number of police cars entered the depot premise and a harsh male voice came out a megaphone which instructed them to surrender.

"Game over." cursed Peter.

August 14th, 10:04 PM

Shobha came back to her police station residence. On the way back to her police station, she had informed all her higher officials about the evening incidence and she specially emphasized on the political angle of that incident.

She entered her living room and searched for a light bulb switch like a blind person. She found one but there was no light in that area and electricity inverter had also given up. She cursed the electricity department and searched for a match box and a candle. She found them lying on her study table. She lit the candle and she saw a familiar man sitting in a chair near her bed. She pulled out her gun, but the man sitting in the chair acted fast his silencer laden gun hissed and the bullet from it struck her gun out of her hand.

"Calm down, dear Shobha." said the man.

"What the hell are you doing here Jafar, did someone gave you contract to kill me? asked Shobha and tried to hide the pain in her hand.

"No darling just came here for a little chit chat." said Jafar with a wicked smile.

"Come to the point or get out of here."

"You've always been a crazy woman; don't you have a little brain to understand that I didn't take all the trouble to come here just to have a look of your filthy face."

She clenched her teeth and said, "Okay, what is it?"

"Where is that woman you caught this evening?"

"We had nothing against her, we let her go."

"Where?"

"At the bus stand."

"Okay, you must have frisked her, what did you find?"

"Why, what's your problem? Go find her and check what she has with her."

"Simple question requires a simple answer, don't make it complicated." said he, and raised his gun and fired again.

The bullet scratched her ear lobe and a little blood dripped out. There was panic on her face, she was sitting in front of the world's most ruthless killer, and she must handle this lunatic delicately.

"Just her personal belongings and her jail discharge certificate." said Shobha.

"That's better now, let's move ahead now, did she have any weapon with her?"

"No, there was no weapon in her bag."

"Any idea, where she is heading to?"

"No."

"Don't you think you are getting older and flabby?"

"Put the gun down, you'll know who is getting flabby."

"Interesting." said he, and put his gun down on the floor.

The moment he put his gun down, Shobha darted at the candle and put it off.

There was darkness in the room now. Shobha knew she was not safe in this room so she started moving towards the room door. She outstretched her arm towards the door, but instead the wooden door her hand touched the rock-hard chest of Jafar. And a powerful blow on her face hurls her in the air and she fell on the floor with some furniture of the room.

There was a gas lighter light in the room which illuminated the face of that ruthless killer near her.

"You have gone flabby dear." whispered Jafar, "Now a little business talk, where has that woman gone?"

"I don't know." said Shobha with remorse. She could feel the killer's hot breath on her face. The moment words fluttered from her mouth; she felt the cold muzzle of the gun below on her belly.

"No more games, deary." Jafar chewed his words. "Open up now otherwise you are a dead duck in a jiffy."

"There was a paper piece in her satchel…."

"Okay, go on."

"JACK was written on that paper."

"JACK." repeated Jafar.

She saw Jafar was a bit away from her, she knew if she didn't act fast the man would certainly kill her. She acted fast and slapped hard on his lighter holding hand, kicked in the belly of Jafar and jumped towards the door. She was very close to the door when a big knife struck her back which forced her down on the floor. She felt unbearable pain between her ribs and she vomited blood on the floor. She used all her power to turn around. The room was lit well, perhaps the light has come or something was burning in her room. She saw the killer was standing near her and wiping her blood from the big knife with her bed sheet. And there was darkness everywhere the next moment.

August 14th, 10:15 PM

Joya was not happy with what they show in prime time. Whatever they show has been telecasted thousands of times. Same old story of an illicit relationship between two people went sour and resulted a few accidental deaths and an attack on the honorable minister. The TRP was not very encouraging; she needed more on this story. Suddenly her cell phone rang, she pressed the call button.

"Go ahead…...the holdup…...okay……did they get her?..........the attackers are arrested……."

She went on talking for a few more minutes and blurted, "Try to film both the places and send videos to the studio.

She ran towards the managing editor room, she entered his room without knocking it and said, "Sir, we have got a breaking news, some people tried to kill a woman near Devdurg."

"You mean the woman might be Seema?"

"I'm sure she was, the attackers have been arrested by the Devdurg police."

"Where is Seema?"

"I've asked Shukla to get a clue on her and tell us as soon as possible. Should we run this breaking news?"

"Yes, we should, but be careful we don't have to sour our relation with the state government also."

"I'll manage that." said she, and she ran towards the telecasting room.

August 14th, 10:30 PM

DIG Shahil Khan was in his study going through some paper work, when the LED TV started running a breaking news.

TWO THUGS TRIED TO KILL A WOMAN NEAR DEVDURG, WOMAN ESCAPED BUT THE THUGHS WERE ARRESTED BY POLICE

Shahil took a few moments to look at the breaking news. As he saw the news for a while and his eyes narrowed. He reached for his cell phone and searched for SSP Devdurg's number which he found after a little search and he dialed the number.

"How are you Khan sir?" said the voice from the other end.

"I'm fine Shekhar, what is the story behind this woman attack scenario."

"I don't have much of this story, one of our SHOs informed me about it, she let the woman go, but the attackers were later arrested by SHO city on behalf of a call given by an anonymous roadways employee.

"Did someone interrogate the attacker?"

"Yes, they didn't tell anything yet. Why are you so curious, is there something behind this incident?"

"Not sure, please let me know if the attackers open up."

"Sure, I'll." And the cell phone screen went blank.

Shahil tilted back and put his head on the cushion of his chair.

There is something big behind this hold up. Devdurg is the junction city between Junagarh and Veer Nagar, Seema might be coming back to Veer Nagaer via Devdurg. And someone tried to get her killed in between the two cities.

He called up SHO city and CO City and instructed them employee sufficient force on the parade ground and snipers on the adjacent buildings.

He also called up PAC commanding officer Rana to employee two section of PAC at the parade ground. He wanted no trouble in his city.

He pondered over the illicit relationship angle and frowned.

August 14th, 10:45 PM

Jafar left the city of Devdurg after killing Shobha, he wanted to get more information from her before killing her. But that woman was too anxious to get herself killed. He stopped his car in front of a roadside motel to have dinner. He ordered Dhal and Chapati with green salad. Suddenly he glanced over his right hand, there were some blood stains left on the side of his palm. He went to the washroom and tried to wash the blood stains with the help of a dirty soap lying on the wash basin. He did his best, but the blood stain didn't go completely. He frowned; he hated to use knives to kill someone. He came back; the waiter had placed his order on his table. He thanked the waiter and started eating.

He was frustrated for not getting any leads on that woman, Seema.

Those two idiots' hasty act had alerted her and she might be anywhere now.

He couldn't get much from Shobha.

Perhaps she tried to fool him, who knows?

Jafar was restless over the words scribbled on the paper.

JACK, what does that stand for? What is the meaning

of these abbreviations? Is it a name or a code word or simply a gimmick by Shobha or that woman to fool others?

Does that word stand for that fool 'Jack,' who pretends to protect the Colonel Pass from criminals? Is she planning to get help from Jack? What if she gets Jack involved in this? Things might go wrong; he may be a problem.

He finished his dinner, paid the bill and came out of the motel. His only clue to trace that woman was, searching her in Will City or at Colonel Pass. He started his car and raced it towards Will City.

August 14th, 11:55 PM

The cab left her at the Dudha check post; the outer police check post which links Will City to the Neva town via Colonel Pass. She let the driver go to a nearby hotel to have his dinner and requested him to come back as soon as possible. Both the places had a contradictory relationship between them. Will City the emerging cosmopolitan city, full of modern marvels, tall buildings, big shopping malls, and night clubs and so on. On the other hand, Neva town, actually not a town, but a collection of five little towns which were parts of the golden triangle. These towns were scattered on a 27 km long agriculture stripe. There were big farm houses bought by rich people from the whole country, but mainly from northern India and Will City. Those farms were mainly leisure, places for the rich people. They spent their lazy hours living in those cozy farm houses and enjoy the peaceful country life. Some Yoga and meditation teachers have established their ashram (hermitages) with five-star facilities. They teach Yoga and Meditation to the rich folks and charge them heavily for their services. All these activities in that area keep the Colonel Pass busy whole the year. There has always been traffic on the pass which keeps the police busy to look after the safe passage of the traffic.

There were some tea vending shops which were still open at this hour. Several insects were hovering around the dimly lit light bulbs. There were some supply trucks, which were being lined up by some police constable to form a convoy. Some of the truck drivers were sitting on the long benches, placed in front the tea shops. There were some cots as well, some empty and some were occupied by the tea shop workers and tired drivers. There was not a single female around. She felt awkward when she looked around; she waited for a moment and then went towards the tea shop. She saw the tea vendor was pouring tea into small glass tumblers.

She went to him and asked, *"Bhai jee Jack Saab kaha milenge?"*(Brother, where could Mr. Jack be found?)

The tea vendor was surprised to see a woman at this hour, he looked at her from tip to toe and answered, *"Bahenjee Jack Saab karwa ke peeche ayenge."* (Sister Mr. Jack will come trailing the convoy.)

She sat down on a deserted bench's corner. She put her small satchel on the bench; there was little sound which was made by the metal and wood's contact. She looked around; there was not a single soul who was interested in that sound. There was a heavy locally made revolver in her satchel, which she bought just for twenty-five thousand from a grey market dealer in outer Will City. His reference was also given by Devyani. She travelled to Will City to meet Mr. Jack. Devyani, her fellow inmate had told her several times that the man was a living legend. She told her several stories regarding his valor. How he lost his wife and little daughter in the wilderness of the river Kali valley, how he saved several people from the claws of vicious criminals.

She advised her to meet him in any difficult situation, he would certainly help her. And this was the hour of need; there were killers who were looking for her to kill her.

Three and half years was a long time at Zaura, to break an ordinary human being soul. But Seema was living with a hope to get someday out of jail and take her revenge from that beast Ranjeet. She was sure that Ranjeet will also try to kill her and he had acted first.

She observed that Ranjeet always goes in public to hoist the national flag on the Independence Day and the Republic Day. There will be tight security, there will be his private goons and he will also be armed. She hasn't got any clear plan to get near him to shoot him. But it will be her last chance to get her revenge; however, she wasn't sure that she will be left alive to make an attempt on Ranjeet life. She knew there would be more killers on their way to search her and kill her. Though Devyani had advised her to go directly to Jack at Will City's outer check post, but she wasn't sure if that man would help her or not.

A sharp honk brought her back from her somnolence. There were several vehicles which were reaching at the end of Colonel Pass from the Neva side. She waited for the last vehicle to go and then she saw there was coming an age-old green jeep.

August 15, 12:15 AM

Ranjeet Dev was not very happy with what happened in Devdurg. The woman was still alive and his men had been arrested by local police. He had called up his government's minister for internal affairs, to get his men out of the police lock up; they may be broken under the pressure of police.

The minister assured him that his men shall be out of police custody within an hour.

There was still no word from Jafar.

That man was really lunatic. He wouldn't tell him his whereabouts and expect him to rely on him. The man charges a lot of money, the man is really very unpredictable.

His wife had gone to sleep, but he was still waiting for any news from Jafar. He again switched on the TV. To his surprise there was breaking news, the news anchor was shouting to tell the world that a female police officer was brutally murdered by an unknown killer at Devdurg. In the background there was a building enveloped in darkness and a little insufficient light was indicating that the building was a police station.

May be the murdered police officer was the one who forced his men to flee from that culvert. Perhaps Jafar has done this Job to get some information that woman. He is really a very dangerous man, but he really knows what he is doing. May be useful in future also.

But why the hell didn't he get that woman yet?

He cursed that he'll again have to go to parade ground to hoist the flag.

Damn it, I hate going to those public places. But as he was the only government minister in these areas so he has to go there to do this boring work.

He had cautioned all his men to be careful at the parade ground. He has never relied on the useless police force. The new recruits were useless; he'd often use four letters word to curse those police officers.

Damn it, where the hell is that useless Jafar? What has he done? Where the hell is that dangerous woman?

He looked at the wall clock and cursed again.He'll have to hoist the flag at 08:15 AM.

Why the hell this clock is moving so fast.

He went to the nearby wooden cabinet and brought a Black Dog bottle out, poured into a glass tumbler added some water and started sipping it. The twenty-one years old scotch took him into its grip and he went on drinking it until the bottle was empty. His eyes were hazy and his steps were not steady, he walked slowly to his bedroom and fell into his bed.

August 15th, 12:30 AM

The constable took the money from Peter, which he had withdrawn from the ATM situated on the outer ring road of Devdurg. And he left without saying a word.

"Police, my foot…. gang of robbers." snarled Peter.

"How much did you pay?" asked Jagir and drove the car forward.

"Forty thousand, the bloodsuckers, he was adamant on eighty thousand, but I said that was all I had and he took that sum." said Peter and heaved.

Peter was surprised when the Inspector informed him that there were no charges against them so they were free to go. He knew that the minister had pulled some strings, that is why that lion had become a lamb. The inspector took them in his office and offered tea which they declined. But then that filthy mouth demanded the sum of hundred thousand for their immediate release. Peter was surprised that the inspector had a little fear of the politicians who forced him to release them. Peter negotiated and forced him down to forty thousand. In the course of time he has learned not to mess with the police.

"Where to go?" said Jagir.

Peter thought for a while and blurted, "Back to Veer Nagar, we have to face Ranjeet Saab."

August 15th, 12:47 AM

Jafar drove his luxury car very fast to Will City and within two hours he was in the suburb areas of this city. He looked at his GPS and raced towards the direction of Colonel Pass.

This was the first time in his life when he was still searching for his target.

JACK, the legendary warrior, the real pain in the neck.

He never had dreamed to cross paths with that lunatic old man. He has searched everything about him available on the net. The man was really a dangerous one, fastest gunslinger. Does that woman know him? What will be the outcome if Jack stands against him?

What the hell, he was just imagining things. To the hell this legendary warrior, he'll breathe last if he dares to cross paths with him.

He reached on the Dudha check post. There were several commercial vehicles lined up to go to the golden triangle area.

He looked around; there was no sign of that woman. He saw there were some tea vending shops on the other side of the road. Let's give a try out there as well. He came out of his car; left it unlocked and crossed the rough road. He went close to the shops and tried to trace that woman in the dimly lit outer area of the shops. There were several truck drivers having tea and soft drinks, but there was still not a sign of that woman.

He cursed his luck and looked around again through the darkness. Suddenly the dark area bathes into the light from the approaching vehicle's headlights. And then he saw her. She was there; sitting on a corner bench, looking in the direction of coming vehicles. He put his right hand inside his shirt and felt the cold handle of his magnum, placed in the shoulder holster.

Suddenly a police car emerged from the pass and policemen came out of it and scattered everywhere. He pulled out his hand and stood there for a while and after a few moments he returned to his car. He will have to wait for a better chance. He cannot afford to lose this woman now; he'll have to be extra careful. Staying at this place for a long time was also not possible, it was a police check post, there may be policemen who may come and search his full of weapons car.

He'll have to leave this place. He started his car and started moving in the direction of the city. Soon he found what he was looking for, there was a man-made mound of debris. He stopped his car and took his sniper gun out of the bag and fixed an infrared telescope on it and checked it, he could see everything through its green light.

He came out of his car crossed the road carefully, there was not a single soul looking at him at this hour. He carefully mounted up on the mound; it was at least thirty feet high. He was using only his instincts to move up side, one wrong step and he will go down with a thud.

Finally, he got up on the top of the mound and looked for a perfect place to have a look at the check post tea vending shops. He found one and lies down on the rough ground. He placed the gun in correct position and peeped through the scope, there was sort of commotion on the check post.

He saw the woman was standing now and walking towards a tall man. He looked at the bony face of that thin man.

Yes; he was the legendary warrior, Jack, the lunatic Jack.

He moved his gun slowly and fixed it on the head of that woman.

August 15th, 12:50 AM

Seema looked at the approaching open jeep. The driver of the jeep was still in the dark; his face was not visible yet.

"Behan ji, Jack Saab ki jeep." (Sister, Mr. Jack's Jeep) informed the tea vendor.

Seema looked at the vendor and nodded. The jeep finally came to halt and a tall and thin figure came out of that jeep. His face was still in the dark; he bent down and checked the front tire of the jeep.

Seema got up, picked her satchel up and went straight to the standing jeep.

She looked at the man and blurted, "Good morning sir, may I talk to you?"

The man turned towards her and she had a glimpse of his bony face. His hair was short, gray and dry.

"Sure, what do you want?" asked the man and came a little forward.

She retreated a little and looked at that tall man. He was an old man; he was dressed in loose cotton shirt and trouser. His long hunting shoes were full of dust.

"Sir, I've released from Zoura today, people are chasing to kill me. Sir Minister Ranjeet killed my husband and my little son, he ruined everything I had. The courts were all fixed, they found him innocent. The courts labeled me a characterless woman. I have no faith in those courts, I've come to you in a hope to get the justice served." said Seema with a haste, there were tears in her eyes.

He saw at her with his frigid eyes, turned his face towards the tea shop and said her, "Please follow me."

"Aao Jack Saab, idhar se aao Saab." (Come Mr. Jack, please come this way) said the tea vendor. He moped a dirty table with a damp cloth and blasted the dust from the chairs with the help of a duster.

Jack offered her a seat and occupied one in front of her. The vendor seemed anxious to please Jack, he brought a thermo flask and two bone chine cups. He placed the cups on the table and poured tea from the flask.

"Aapki pasandida chai saab." (Your favorite tea sir) said the tea vendor and stood beside them.

"Thank you, Jogi." said Jack in his rough but calm voice.

The vendor stood there for a while and left.

"Who is chasing you?" asked Jack.

August 15th, 12: 55 AM

Jafar was feeling uneasy, there were several sharp stones mixed with the debris he was laying upon them. But his grip over his gun was steady. He looked through the infrared scope, they were out there in open, but there were some drivers and cleaners who were still walking everywhere and hindering his view.

"Damn it." he said to himself and tried to keep his head clear.

He saw that they were now walking towards the tea shop and he tried to correct the angle of his rifle in their direction. Soon they were inside the tea shop, out of his view. He cursed silently but kept his cool.

You have to be passive in such a situation, be passive,

and keep your head clear...

Fifteen minutes passed, but there was not a sign of them.

August 15th, 01:10 AM

She told him all, she faced all the day.

He listened to her carefully and then spoke in his hoarse voice, "What do you want me to do?"

"Please help me finish that beast off." she said with remorse.

"Who told you that I help people to take their revenge?"

"None, I heard your reputation as a protector of innocent people."

Jack kept quiet for a while and said, "I think there is nothing I can do for you in this matter, besides, if you need anything please tell me, I'll arrange that for you."

Seema looked at the blank face of that so-called legendary warrior. How wrong was she to come to this man, he's declined her request and asking if he could do anything for her?

Hypocrite.

She wiped her half-dried tears and said, "Nothing, sir. Thanks a lot for your time." She got up went straight to the tea vendor.

"Chai ka kitna hua bahiya?" (How much for the tea?)

The tea vendor looked at her and then looked at Jack, who shook his head in disapproval.

The vendor grinned and said, *"Kuch nahi behn ji, ho gaya."* (Nothing sister.)

Seema pulled out a fifty rupee note from his purse, put it on the counter of the shop and came out of the shelter of the tea shop.

August 15th, 01:15 AM

Jafar saw that woman had come out of the shop and there was not a single soul outside the shop now but she.

He fixed the cross wire of his guns telescope on her head and pulled the trigger. Suddenly his mobile phone vibrated.

Damn it…...

01:15:20 AM

Jack saw the woman going out of the shop, his eyes followed her for a while and he also stood up to leave. The convoy was about to proceed.

He just came out of the shop, and then he heard a strange sound.

Swooooosh……...

He saw a bullet hit the shop wall and scratched down some loose plaster from it.

"Lie down!" he shouted and he pulled out his Colt Magnum 44 revolver.

He darted at slowly walking Seema, jumped over her and pulled her down with him and fired three perfect shots in the direction of a firefly which was probably an indicator of an infrared scope.

01:15:22 AM

The vibration of the phone distracted him and he missed his target. He aimed again and fired, but that devil Jack came out of the shop pulled down that woman with him and fired in his direction. He knew the game was over now and he will have to escape.

All the three bullets hit their targets first bullet smashed the barrel of his rifle and other two bullets ripped his arms, perhaps out of their armpits.

He cried in pain, tried to get up, but his arms gave up and came down, tumbling from the mound of the debris.

The devil hasn't killed him, but he wounded him fatally. He collected all his strength and got up his arms were hanging loose. He saw there was a pickup truck coming from the other direction; he ducked down in the dark. The truck was his only chance, he waited until the truck passed before him, he recollected all his strength again and moved his right arm and held the iron chain hanging at the truck haul. He dragged with the truck for a while and then he jumped like a rubber puppet, and the next moment he was lying in the empty truck haul. The mission failed and he was badly wounded.

That devil of a man had failed him, failed him for the first time in his life and wounded him.That man was a pro, he wounded him deliberately, he would have killed him. The man was a real devil, he doesn't need infrared to look through the darkness of night, he could shoot anything with his bare eyes through darkness. That man is a true menace, he must die.

The truck was moving towards Will City and Jafar was pulling out his revolver to take over it. Who knows, the police or that devil may come after him trailing his blood smell.

August 15th, 01:25 AM

"Who the hell fired?" came the Dudha police check post in charge shouting; there were a few constables who followed him. He looked around and saw, Jack was standing there with a revolver in his hand and a woman was lying on the ground.

"What the hell is going on here?" said the in charge looking at Jack suspiciously.

And that very time another bullet smashed a truck's front screen with an ear deafening sounded. The in charge heard the sound and he ran towards the shelter of his police check post along with his constables.

Jack gave a hand to Seema and helped her to get on her feet. She hadn't come to her sense yet, she was surprised to see the agility of the man standing beside her. He was still alert and staring through the darkness.

"Come with me." said he, and moved towards his jeep.

Seema stood there standstill.

Jack looked back at her perplexed.

"There is a danger to your life here, please come with me, I'll leave you at any safe place." said Jack.

"There is no safe place for me in this world, they are after me, they won't rest until they kill me. There were two attempts on my life during the last twelve hours. I'm surprised how they missed me? I've never been afraid of death; I'll kill that beast Ranjeet anyhow or die trying." retorted Seema.

The police check post in charge came out of his hiding place and looked at the two people standing alone in the open area. He swept sweat drops from his forehead and pulled out his service revolver from its holster and targeted it towards Jack.

"Jack, you have crossed your limits this time, you are firing in front of police and endangering innocent peoples' lives, you are under arrest, I won't spare you this time."

shouted the in charge looking sheepishly around.

"Don't worry Daga, whoever fired at us must have fled so far, send your men to check it out. And as far as your wish to arrest me, is concerned, please keep it away for a while, because I'm also a citizen of this country and have my right to protect myself from the gunslingers. Perhaps that is why government granted me this weapon license. But if someone files a complaint against me, I'll come myself to you to prove my innocence." retorted Jack.

Daga was about to say something, a highway patrol car pulled in with the screeching sound siren. The car stopped in front of them and subdivision Circle Officer (CO) of Police appeared from it. All the police constables and the check post in charge saluted him.

"What's going on Daga?" CO asked from the check post in charge.

Daga explained everything.

"What did you do to seek that gun man?"

"Sir, I'm going myself after that man."

"Be sincere Daga, I won't bear more foolishness, I want that gunman at any rate, got it?"

"Yes sir!" said Daga and left with his men.

CO turned towards jack and shook hand with him and said, "What was all that Jack sir?"

"I don't know, someone started shooting here, I fired in response."

CO thought for a moment and said, "I don't believe Daga, I'll personally look for that gunman." And he left.

Jack looked around there was no sign of that girl, she had gone.

Jack fished out his cell phone and called up Raut, his farm manager and started giving him instructions.

August 15th, 01:35 AM

Seema saw all the brawl and saw that the police in charge might arrest her along with that gun fighter Jack. She decided to leave at that very moment.

She slipped off stealthily and started moving fast towards the cab which was still waiting for her. She entered the cab and told the driver to go to Veer Nagar.

That man Jack is really a daredevil, he lives up to his name, the legendary warrior. She was surprised to see the way he forced her down to the ground and shoot simultaneously. No one knew what happened to the assailant, whether he'd fled or killed. But one thing was sure that Jack took him by surprise and outwitted him.

She checked her satchel; the revolver was safe.

August 15th, 02:00 AM

The truck driver has realized that there was an injured man lying on the haul of his truck, but the man also had a gun in his hand, a very dangerous situation for him. The man was bleeding profusely; there was blood all over the haul.

"Ramu, we are in danger, there is a man lying in the haul with a gun." he said to the cleaner.

"*Ustad* (Master), let's get rid of this stolen truck.

"You are right, let's run this truck into Kali River and jump off."

"Great, we'll do it."

Soon the long bridge of river Kali was dimly visible. And the driver pushed the gas paddle to increase the speed of the truck. The driver took an iron rod and fixed it between the steering and the driver seat of the truck that the truck could run straight. Then he signaled his cleaner to jump off and they jumped from the truck simultaneously. They hit the concrete road and their bodies rolled on the road before they gained any sense. They saw the truck was running towards the river bank and after a few moments the truck broke the brick railing and went straight into the stream of the river.

The driver was very sad to see the truck going straight in the river.

"Phew, a narrow escape!" exclaimed the driver.

"Ha ustaad bach gaye." (Yes, master we are safe now) said the cleaner.

"Who said it to you?"

A third voice echoed in the atmosphere and the man in the haul was standing in front of them with a gun targeted towards them.

"You idiots, tried to kill me, now it's the time for you to die." Jafar chewed his words.

"Sorry sir, the truck was out of control, we ourselves jumped from the truck to save our lives." blurted both of them in unison.

"I believe you both, now stop a passing vehicle."

"Sure, sir, we'll do it."

Jafar was feeling very week, the constant loss of blood making him dizzy. He sensed the danger when the driver increased the speed of the truck and he jumped off the haul before the driver and the cleaner of the truck. Now they were both trying to take a lift from the passing vehicles. None seem to care about the filthy looking driver and cleaner. But suddenly a car stopped and Jafar ran towards it, he pulled open the rear door of the car and entered.

"Who are you, what do you want?" said the elderly looking driver.

"I'm injured, sir, please take me to a surgeon." said

Jafar with a lot of effort and flashed the gun before the face of the car driver.

The car driver understood and started moving slowly. The driver and the cleaner didn't make any effort to enter the car.

"Please move fast, I need medical care badly."

The driver pushed the gas paddle to increase the speed of the car.

August 15th, 05:00 AM

DIG Shahil Khan had a very little sleep at the night and the little sleep he had; was full of nightmares. He got up at 04:00 AM, got through his daily routine had a cup of tea. He went through all the information his allies collected on Seema all through the night, but there was nothing remarkable. There was no news about the whereabouts of Seema. She had vanished suddenly.

He went through the news of Killing of a police officer in Devdurg, the shootout at Colonel Pass. He talked to the SSPs of both the districts, but they also had no answers to his questions. Will City police tried to trace that gunman, but without any success. He tried to put all these events together, but there wasn't any possible connection between all these events. The flag hoisting ceremony on the parade ground was about to take place between 07:00 to 09:00 AM. All he could do was to tighten the security of the minister at the parade ground.

He called up all his sub inspectors to follow him to the parade ground.

August 15th, 05:30 AM

Peter was not happy to see the early morning light at Veer Nagar, he instructed Jagir to drive to his outer city den where he kept all the weapons he often uses.

They crossed Airport Boulevard and took the outer ring road towards the Lumira Colony, where his den was situated in an isolated alley. The den was actually a duplex which was leased in the name of his wife and he used to keep all his illegal weapons there.

Jagir stopped the car in the porch of the den.

"Want to drink something?" said he to Jagir.

"I'm dead tired, I need something strong, very strong." said Jagir with a big yawn.

"Gone crazy, we don't have time to get booze over our heads, we need to work all the day. I know that crazy woman; she'll not miss a single chance to kill the minister. I'm dead sure our reunion with that woman will be in this city, and I have to wipe her off before showing my face to the minister. So, go ahead and make a strong coffee for both of us, you'll find the coffee powder and dry milk in the upper cabinet of the kitchen." retorted Peter.

"As you wish boss," said Jagir with a little irritation.

August 15th, 06:45 AM

The booze had taken over Ranjeet's head, but he couldn't sleep at all but kept tossing in the bed until his wife announced that it was time to get up.

He cursed her silently and got up. Soon his wife served breakfast on the table for which he had no appetite. He sipped the hot coffee and tried Jafar's number, which was obviously out of service area right now. He also tried Peter number, but there was no answer from the other end.

Then he called up Mukhiya, his henchman to his residence to accompany him to the parade ground. He was supposed to on the parade ground at 07:30 to hoist the national flag at 07:40 AM.

What the hell should I do? Why the hell should I hoist the flag? I need a break; someone please give me a break. There is a killer outside looking for me. I haven't touched a woman outside of my marriage since that fateful day. Oh, what the hell, where has all my killers gone? Why don't they comfort me with the news of her death? Useless bloodsuckers! Why the hell didn't I get her killed at Zoura?

"What are you murmuring is there a problem?" said his wife, looking at his face.

"No, nothing, please leave me alone." he barked at his wife.

His wife looked at him with disgust and left the dining room.

He looked at his wrist watch, time to leave. He came out and saw that Mukhiya and his men were waiting for him at the porch.

Mukhiya, a tall and strong man, was looking at the private security of the minister. He was a man of great strength and was well versed with every weapon. His men were also ruthless killers. Ranjeet indicated him to get into his car and sit beside him. Mukhiya followed his order and suddenly a sub inspector came running towards the car and said, "Sir, I'm supposed to travel with you to the parade ground."

"Daroga ji, minister saab ki security aaj hum dekhenge, tum peeche peeche aao." (We'll look after the security of the minister today, you better come trailing us.)

In the name of love

said Mukhiya.

Sub inspector looked at the minister helplessly. The minister nodded in approval and he ran towards the police car to follow the convoy of the minister and his men.

Soon they were on the roads of Veer Nagar. The heat outside was unbearable it might rain today.

August 15th, 06:55 AM

DIG Khan, took a quick tour of the parade ground. He ensured that all the snipers were at their places and alert.

He briefed all the police units that there may be some killers to attack the minister. Make sure there should be no armed man inside the parade ground, no matter the man is with the minister or not. Take special care of any single woman who comes near the parade ground. There should be no unknown face in or around the parade ground.

"But there are several women members of ruling party who are participating in the program." informed Deepak, the sub inspector at district headquarter.

"Ugh, that is a big problem." said Khan and called up the IG.

The IG was frustrated, he barked like a mad dog, "Look Khan, if anything happens to minister, I'll take it personally and won't let you go with it."

"I'll make it sure that the minister reaches his home safely." said Khan and let the screen of his cell phone went blank.

"Deepak, where are the female party workers? I want to have a word with them."

"Come with me, sir."

There were at least twenty female workers who were clad in pink cotton sarees. They were all gathered at the parade ground gate with flower garlands to welcome their leader. Khan looked at them carefully; they were all in their late twenties or earlier thirties.

"Do you all know each other?" said Khan, looking at them with his piercing eyes.

"Yes, we do." said an elderly looking woman, but there was no confidence in her voice.

Khan sensed that and said, "Won't you mind if our female officers frisked you?" said Khan to her.

"Not at all officer, we are ready to do anything for our leader." chirped the elderly lady.

"Kamal, get it done immediately, the minister is about to come."

"Okay, sir." said Kamal and he waved all the female police officers and constables to come.

Soon the female officers hoarded all the female workers to a close tent where they started frisking them. And that very moment someone shouted outside that the minister's car was approaching.

August 15th, 07:25 AM

Zoya and her crew were reporting live from the parade ground. She was reporting diligently, but her eyes were darting here and there in search of any suspicious person who might attack the minister. She was describing the weather which was very hot and humid at this time. The sky was overcast and it was likely to rain. She looked at the sky and went on reporting.

Suddenly DIG Khan appeared on the parade ground and looked at the NEWS people; he almost knew everybody and he greeted them.

Zoya rushed towards him with her crew. Soon both of them were face to face. Khan was preoccupied so he tried to wave her off, but her cameraman focused his camera on DIG.

"Sir, I saw there is a lot of force all over this parade ground, there are some snipers who are deployed on the roofs the adjoining buildings. Is there any danger to minister's life?"

"Not at all, this is just a routine practice to avoid any miss happening."

"Can you kindly tell us something about Seema's menace?"

"What menace? You news people are really inventors of new terms."

"You are avoiding my question."

"Not at all, there is no menace."

"Don't be so sure, sir, you know Seema has been released from the jail and she may attack again."

"I'm not sure that the woman will dare to come here, if she comes here, we have enough force to take care of her."

"Okay, sir, by the way, if she comes and attack the minister, what will you do? Arrest her or shoot her?"

"I'm not sure that she'll ever come near this parade ground, but if she dares, I'll handle her firmly."

"Means, you are going to shoot her at sight."

"Did I say so?"

"I understand your intentions, take care officer the TV media will be looking at you closely."

"I know, please excuse me now."

And that very moment the sound of a hooter announced that the minister has arrived.

Zoya looked at the convoy of cars coming close to the main entrance of parade ground.

And all of a sudden it started raining.

August 15th, 07:30 AM

Seema took her garland and rushed towards the main entrance. She has wrapped the garland all over the revolver. Devyani had informed her that there shall be some female party workers to welcome the minister; they always wear pink cotton saree and pink cotton blouse. She has already bought the dress at Junagarh and there was no problem mingling with the pink clad party workers at the parade ground. But the police officer had put her really in a fix by ordering to frisk all the female workers. But the announcement of minister's arrival ignited all the female workers and they all ran towards the main entrance of the parade ground to welcome their minister with garlands.

Suddenly the garland slipped from her hands and fell on the ground and the metal sound alerted the security guards.

"What was that? Stop!" screamed the security guard.

She didn't heed him, she tore the garland and took the revolver in her hand unlocked it while running towards the main entrance of the ground.

The distance between the security room and the main entrance was 100 yards; she was running like a mad woman. The first gust of heavy rain damped her clothes and her hair.

The security guard alerted all the police force and now there were several policemen running behind her. Some of them took their position on the damp ground and fired, but the rain and public on the ground distracted them, they cursed themselves.

Khan heard the commotion outside the security room, but the rain was hindering his view. The women were all over the minister who was standing under a big umbrella and was accepting their garlands. Khan felt uneasy, there was something wrong and all of a sudden, a pink clad woman came running towards the main entrance. She had a big revolver in her hand; Khan looked at her through the heavy rain. And his hand moved towards his service pistol automatically.

August 15th, 07:35 AM

Seema came towards the main entrance running and she saw the women crowd around the minister and she shouted in a high pitch voice.

"Hat Jao, Aaj tu marega Ranjeet," (Clear the way, Ranjeet, you'll die today)

Her hoarse voice took the women's attention and all of them saw a woman standing there with a revolver in her hand. All of them screamed and scattered and now Seema and Ranjeet were face to face and then Seema fired. First bullet smashed the face of the minister and other bullets bounced back from his bullet proof vest. The minister fell like a heavy tree and the blood from his face started changing the color of the rain water.

Khan raised his gun, but a fleeing woman clashed with him and both of them fell entwined. He saw through the rain that the minister had fallen dead and the killer woman was standing there with a hope to see any sign of life in him.

Mukhiya and his men saw the fall of the minister with a fear and they raised their weapons at her direction.

All the policemen came running towards the main entrance and were mesmerized to see the minister's dead remains. Some of them shouted, "Shoot her."

They came out of the shock and started firing in her direction. But all of a sudden,an LPG gas tanker came crashing all the cars and police vehicles standing before the parade ground. All the bullets smashed on the heavy metal body of the tanker. The tanker driver lost control and then smashed it in the main entrance of the ground. The snipers were also firing but their bullets could kill other people at the ground so they decided to stop firing.

Khan was standing like a fool; his gun was hanging in his loose hand. The truck had hindered the entrance of the ground. It had smashed all the police vehicles.

Zoya was mesmerized to see the pink clad Seema, she was a real beauty and the man lying dead had snatched all the happiness of her life. She saw the gas truck was leaking now and the people were running all over to escape from the gas. It was raining heavily when a white van came screeching it brakes. The side door of the van splits open and a hand dragged Seema into the van and the van was gone in a few seconds.

Shahil Khan

IG Jeevan Anand cursed Khan for his incompetency to save a state minister. He even used four letter words, he personally called up the chief minister and forced him to suspend Khan immediately and start a departmental inquiry against him. Khan immediately applied for the long leave and left for his home town.

Zoya

The Chief Editor looked at the interview she filmed with DIG Khan, he frowned and abused her.

"This is the interview you want me to telecast; it seems all your sympathy was with that murderer woman. I run this news channel to earn some money and you are ruining my relationship with the government and the chief minister."

"Sir, do I have any right to differentiate between the wrong and the right, do I have any right to show the truth to this country people?"

Chief Editor clenched his teeth and blurted, "The chief minister is my friend and I'll not run a program against his dead minister and his government. Let me tell you a truth, there is not a single news channel which could run a program against the dead minister, we will not glorify her."

"Are you a newsman or a government agent?" said Zoya.

"What did you call me? A government agent. Okay, I'm a government agent and you are fired at the very moment. Don't worry; I'll make it sure that no news channel takes you in."

"Thank you, sir, I cannot be a pawn of a corrupt news channel, you don't need to fire me, I'm resigning myself."

"Get out!" shouted the chief editor.

She surrendered all the belongings of the channel, including her cell phone, laptop, tablet computer and office card. She came out of the channel building. It was still raining and there was rain water everywhere. Streets were inundated. She waited for a while and then came out in the rain and walked across the road to take shelter somewhere else.

Seema

Raut managed the escape of Seema from the parade ground, the gas trunk was also a part of his plan. They changed the van with a sedan car after a few km. Seema was sitting silently and her clothes were still full of mud smudges and water was dripping from them.

"Did Mr. Jack send you to help me?"

"Yes, he wanted to get you out of that mess."

"Please thank him for his kindness and now let me go."

"I can leave you wherever you want to go."

"Thank you, I don't need your help anymore, I've committed a murder, I want to surrender."

"The police won't spare you now, they must be looking for you to kill you, the minister was a close friend of the chief minister. They'll kill you in a fake encounter."

"They can't kill me, I'm dead long ago. The corpse was just seeking the revenge, which it took today. Let me go now."

Raut looked at her expressionless face of the woman, shrugged and opened the car door. She went out of the car in the rain, she was walking like zombie. Rout waited until she disappeared in the thick rain.

Peter

The news of the minister's death eased Peter a little, but his mentor was dead now. He'll have to start it all again. He was sort of unemployed now. He was the hammer of the minister and he was looking after all the illegal operations of the minister Ranjeet.

He cursed himself for not killing that woman at the culvert near Devdurg.

"What are you thinking boss?" said Jagir.

"Nothing, just go on driving, that filthy woman has put a question mark on our lives too. If that Julfi comes to power, he will finish us off to control all the operation. Damn it, that woman has really ruined us."

Jagir heard all his cussing; he concentrated on the inundated street. Suddenly he saw a woman walking in the rain; her pink clothes were drenched with water. She was walking like a dead person. Jagir cleaned the car's screen with a newspaper and looked at the almost familiar face of the woman. Yes, she was the one they lost at the culvert.

"Look boss, who is walking in the rain?"

"Who? Okay, good work Jagir, we got her, but unfortunately after losing our mentor." said Peter and pulled out a bowie knife from his long shoe.

"I'll cut her into small pieces." said Peter and jumped out in the rain.

Seema could hardly see anything through the rain, but she went on walking. Suddenly a burly man became visible. The man was walking towards her with a long knife in his hand. He was one of her assailants. She closed her eyes, it was the time to leave this world and meet her husband and her little son in another world, if there was one anywhere. She felt a powerful hand wrapped around her neck and a sharp knife opened her belly. She gulped some rainwater and fell down; her assailant also bent down and went on stabbing her.

Raut moved a little ahead through the thick rain wall. The wiper of his car was wiping rainwater from his front screen. He saw Seema lying on the road and a burly man was stabbing her. He stopped his car and pulled out his gun and ran towards Seema.

"Hey ruffian, leave her alone!" Shouted Raut.

But the man sitting beside Seema pulled out his pistol and fired at Raut. Rout dodged the bullet and fired back. His bullet hit the burly man's broad chest and the man fell down near Seema and started creeping towards a standing car. Raut let him go and looked at Seema, her lifeless eyes were open, but there was no life in them. Raut clenched his jaw and looked at the creeping man. He went near him and aimed at his head and fired and the bullet blasted his head. Suddenly another man came out of the standing car; he also had a gun in his hand.

Raut looked at him with his burning eyes. The man shuddered and his gun fell down from his hands. Raut spat rain water from his mouth and walked towards the dead body of Seema.

Jafar

The surgeon looked at the man lying on the bed. He had to cut both his arms to save his life. The man turned his face from him, perhaps he was weeping. The elderly man thanked the doctor and left the hospital to continue his journey.

The City

It was an extraordinary day for Will City as three dead bodies were brought to city hospital mortuary for the autopsy. The state minister Ranjit Dev, his assailant Seema and an unknown man body were placed in the boxes side by side in the freezing mortuary, all of them equally waiting for the autopsy.

Next day after autopsy Ranjit's body was taken by his family but no one came to claim the remaining bodies. By the afternoon Jack's farm manager Raut claimed the body of Seema and the police who was eager to get rid of her body handed it over to Raut after a little paper work. None came to claim the body the man who was later found to be contract killer; police decided to send it for the electric cremation. It was still raining all the day.

Lonely Pyre

Jack saw the fire flames which were sky high at this moment. The flames were consuming the remains of Seema body. There was no rain at the Pike peak. Jack saw Duke neighed, Raut patted him. it was time to go to protect the convoys from the invisible assailants. He glanced at the pyre last time and went close to his horse, took his reigns from his farm manager Raut and started walking through the labyrinths of the River kali valley. Raut also followed him on his horse.

The lonely pyre was still burning.